NO MORE BOWS

BY SAMANTHA COTTERILL

HARPER

An Imprint of HarperCollinsPublishers

HUGO AND MILLY had been playing tea party . . .
and dress-up . . . and house . . . all morning.
So when Hugo heard: "Time for a walk!"
he was ready to go.

ZIP . . .

ZAP . . .

ZOOM!

What's taking so long? Hugo wondered.

What's this? A bow? Had Milly lost her mind?

Hugo was *not* amused.

But the neighborhood dogs sure were.

Something will have to be done about this horrible bow, thought Hugo.

With a tug . . .

a pull . . .

. . . and a POP!

Hugo managed to get rid of the bow. Phew!

The next day, Milly called, "Hugo! Time for a walk!"

ZIP . . .

ZAP . . .

ZOOM!

Oh no! Hugo was *still* not amused.

But the neighborhood dogs sure were.
And this time they laughed even harder.

Something must be done with this horrible, dreadful bow, thought Hugo.

With a tug . . .

a pull . . .

. . . and a POP!

Hugo got rid of that bow for good . . .
or so he thought.

Then came more bows. Frilly ones. Sparkly ones.
Bows with jewels and bows with buttons.

NO.

SERIOUSLY?

NOPE.

I THINK NOT.

Hugo just couldn't take it any longer.

ARE YOU KIDDING ME?

NO WAY.

OH DEAR NO.

DEFINITELY NOT.

NO MORE BOWS!

Hugo had finally had enough!

NO . . .

MORE . . .

BOWS!

But running off to the city only made
Hugo feel sad and alone.
What have I done? thought Hugo.

On the store sign:

SHOW
your dogs
you ♥
THEM!

And then Hugo noticed something.
A dog with a bow? Looking happy?
And his girl looked happy too?

Hugo was starting to miss Milly.

Back near home, Milly was worried about Hugo.

Hugo couldn't take it any longer. . . .

ZIP . . .

ZAP . . .

ZOOM!

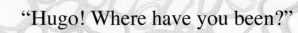

"Hugo! Where have you been?"

Hugo pulled Milly through the city.
They couldn't get there fast enough!

Ta-da! The bow Hugo wanted was neither frilly nor sparkly.

And there were no buttons or jewels.

It was simply the most magnificent bow he had ever seen.

"Excellent find, Hugo! You'll look adorable in that!"

The next day, Hugo and Milly headed out for a walk.
Hugo felt proud as he strutted through town wearing
such a magnificent bow and shiny new boots.

This time, none of the dogs were laughing.

(Well, none except Hugo.)

For my fantastic agent, Kirsten Hall.
One look at a simple doodle about a dog and a bow
and she knew I was meant to write and illustrate picture books.

No More Bows
Copyright © 2017 by Samantha Cotterill
All rights reserved. Manufactured in China. No part of this book may be used or reproduced in any manner whatsoever without
written permission except in the case of brief quotations embodied in critical articles and reviews. For information address
HarperCollins Children's Books, a division of HarperCollins Publishers, 195 Broadway, New York, NY 10007.
www.harpercollinschildrens.com

ISBN 978-0-06-240870-9 (trade bdg.)

The artist used Adobe Photoshop to create the digital illustrations for this book.
Typography by Chelsea C. Donaldson
16 17 18 19 20 SCP 10 9 8 7 6 5 4 3 2 1
❖
First Edition